ALL ABOUT NATURE

By

Jan Michael C. Sotto, MASE, D. Hum

DEDICATION

To my parents, Rafael and Arleta,
who served as my foremost inspiration and who taught
me to believe in the idea that through faith and hard
work, everything is possible;

To my friends,
who motivated me to be at my best both during my
blisses and struggles;

To my wife, Monique,
who always support and genuinely love me and for
always encouraging me most especially during the times
I have almost given up;

To my baby Amari,
who is the source of my happiness,
my inspiration in doing everything;

Above all,
to our Almighty God who is and forever will be the
source of everything.

- JMDCS-

ACKNOWLEDGMENT

First of all, the author is very grateful to the Almighty God for enabling him to finish this book.

Also, this work of art would not have been possible without the help and support of different significant individuals who rendered their time and effort in the preparation and completion of this book.

He wishes to extend his sincere appreciation and gratitude to Monica P. Sotto, his wife, who polished the technical features of the contents of this book.

To Rolaine San Juan, Nemesis Manahan, Carlito Colinares, Jonathan Tungol, and Lyca Balume for their wonderful illustrations about nature which made this book more aesthetically pleasing and interesting.

And finally, the author would like to acknowledge with gratitude, the support, and love of his family and friends. They all motivated him to keep on going, thus everything in this book would not have been possible without them.

-JMDCS

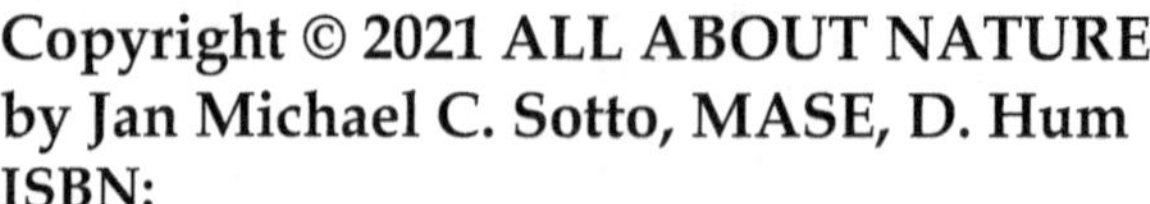

Published by Poetry Planet Book Publishing House
Edited by Marie Ezekiel
Designed by Tess Ritumalta
Illustrations;
"Rebirth" by Rolaine San Juan
"Genesis 9:13" by Rolaine San Juan
"City Lights in Land" by Rolaine San Juan
"Unseen Truth" by Rolaine San Juan
"Genetic Decoding" by Nemesis Manahan
"Wise" by Nemesis Manahan
"BiodiversiFree" by Carlito Colinares
"Predator" by Lyca Balume
"[PAG]dar[ASA] sa Bawat Pagpikit at Pagmulat ng Mata"
by Jonathan Tungol

Some photos used are taken on Pinterest and canva and may contain their copyright.

PREFACE

When writing uses nature as motivation, its scribblings metamorphosize into something really great... For years, writers used nature as their source of inspiration because of its beauty. Infact, millions of books have been created because of it. The author wrote this book to protect nature.

Nature has been taken for granted since the day God threw mankind out of the Garden of Eden. Their source of living, shelter, and everything that benefits them comes from it aside from the fact that it's free. It is God's gift to us showing his unconditional love. We might have an abundance of appreciation for it but have we ever thought of protecting it, to preserve it, to love and take care of it?

The author emphasizes the need to safeguard our nature and also has given pieces of evidence why we should... His book may be simple but it has vivid lessons we all should grasp seriously... Read his book and you will be amazed how he uses poetry to save our earth from devastation: "ALL ABOUT NATURE" is a must-read by all.

TABLE OF CONTENTS

Page

ONE

This chapter contains one-stanza poems themed on biodiversity conservation. Through the simple poems, the public will gain awareness regarding the actions which they need to do to protect and save the environment.

Biodiversity in Its Truest Sense

Biodiversity deals with species
variability,
It boosts the ecosystem's productivity,
It aides on the sustainability of the
natural resources,
It is important for the survival of
wildlife and humanity.

Nature's Purpose

Nature is our life!
It gives us hope, it gives us light.
So, we should not stop with our fight!
Let us protect our environment, day,
and night.

Birds

Look above, birds fly so high,
Confidently, staying calm in the sky,
They seem lovely and gay,
Do not let them vanish, let them stay.

Fish

Fish in the ocean swim so deep,
What a lovely scene to keep,
So, stop coral reef destruction,
Help sea creatures survive for the future
generation.

Flowers

Blue, red, pink, white, orange, and
yellow,
Flowers need to grow!
Let all of them bloom,
Do not let them be gone too soon!

Tree

To solve problems related to our nature,
Remind everyone that planting may be
a cure,
Encourage the youngsters to plant a
tree,
Earth will be protected for you and me.

Perfect Scene

As the rabbits hop in a vibrant plain,
The birds sing in a sweet refrain,
Other animals are playing wild and free,
Truly a perfect scenery to see.

Unanswered Questions

What if the chirp of a bird, bubble of a
fish, or roar of a lion means something?
Are you willing to listen and describe
their meaning?
What if you find that help is what they
are asking?
Are you willing to help them, or you
will just leave them begging?

Just Like Us

We always say that we need to be
protected,
Air, water, foods, and shelter are mainly
what we needed,
Just like us, animals need to be
safeguarded,
They need to be fed, sheltered, and
loved, let us be open-minded.

Caged

What they need is freedom,
Let them live in their own kingdom,
Cage is not the kind of shelter they
need,
Nature is where their comfort is, so let
them be freed.

Poaching

Poaching, Oh what an evil thing!
Stop it and start caring,
Wildlife needs to be protected,
Wildlife deserves to be loved, no to be
hunted.

Empty

What would be nature's picture?
What is Earth without living creatures?
Do you want to live in an empty world?
Protect our environment, be the
threshold.

Leave the Forest Alone

The green forest, leave it alone,
For animals consider it their peaceful
home,
Deforestation is not good at all,
Let us make the act of illegal mining fall.

Fear of Open Season

I am afraid! It is almost open season,
The event is killing me for so many
reasons,
I am begging, spare me a little of your
attention,
Save us for the sake of your future
generation.

If Only

If there is only one thing which I can do,
It is to use my voice to protect plants
and animals too,
Through social media, I will promote
awareness,
Thoughts about wildlife preservation, in
my little way, I will express.

Not Only Us

Tell me what really happened.
Do you really care, or you only
pretended?
Show some concern before everything
will be wasted.
It is not only humans, animals also
deserved to be protected.

Soon

Let the wildflowers bloom,
Let the butterfly get out of its cocoon,
Let the fish swim in the blue lagoon,
Everything in nature will be fine very
soon.

Do Something

Act now before it lasts,
The wildlife deteriorates too fast,
Do something for them to survive.
The future needs to see them alive.

Peace

The stillness of the sea keeps on
reminding us,
The rustling sound of the forest keeps
on telling us,
That animals need to live in peace,
So, let nature may have its peace.

One Step for Future Generation

Wear your slippers, take your first step, explore,
Through your initiative, positive environmental change may occur,
Let the kangaroos hop, let the whales swim, let the eagles soar,
The wildlife of today, helps the future generation see and adore.

Youths for Wildlife Preservation

Youths, the hopes of the ASEAN
nations,
Must step-out and show participation,
Their support may lead to wildlife
preservation,
Their simple acts may save the
environment for the future generation.

Best Time, Now!

You must act now before it is too late,
You can make a change, just believe,
have faith,
Show concern for the wildlife's sake,
Act now, the future is at stake! Soon
everything will be alright.

The Initial Step

Let us start planting trees,
Save the wildlife, I insist!
Mother Earth needs your attention!
Save it now for the future generation!

Fight!

Soon everything will be alright,
Our nature's future will be bright.
Our efforts will be the light.
Never give up, for the wildlife, we will
fight!

Be Brave!

For Earth to be saved,
Let us all act, let us be brave!
Take care of all the creatures,
Protect the Earth and all its features.

Be an Icon!

Be an icon of the future generation,
Make an initiative for wildlife
preservation,
Make a move to create a chain reaction,
That will show cooperation among the
ASEAN nations.

TWO

This chapter contains two-stanza poems which reflect the connection of colors with nature. Each poem focuses on how the symbolism of each color encourages others to do something in saving the Earth.

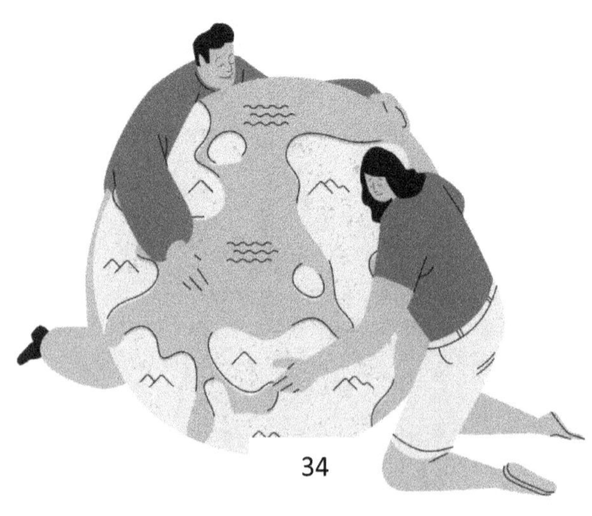

White

The sun shines so brightly.
Giving radiance along with moonlight!
Saying with the hope we hold on tight.

Environment seeks human protection,
From its unacceptable destruction.
We need to go on with our motion,
In saving the Earth for the future generation.

Black

Lifeless!
Do not let yourself be clueless!
All plants and animals are harmless!
Give them life, especially the homeless!

Save endangered species,
Let animals live like water lilies,
Treat all animals like our best buddies,
Even the wildest ones are not our enemies!

Rainbow

Let nature's beauty glow!
Let the water in the river freely flow!
Let the trees in the forest grow!

Let us put colors to nature,
By simply protecting its features.
We can live happily with other creatures,
If we will give our nature a future.

Red

Let the summon of Earth be heard,
She cried, she suffered,
Be brave, help her!

Who will not let her suffer?
Everyone needs her,
Please do not surrender,
Act! It is now or never!

Orange

Do not let the Earth's warmth change,
Make it natural, do not make it strange,
Let it be, do not change its range.

Let us reciprocate her kindness,
She deserves happiness,
She is a true mother to all,
A great provider of all.

Yellow

Let happiness flow!
From running water to falling snow,
From empty soil to seeds that grow.

Sun brings positivity,
It brings hope to humanity,
It provides enough energy,
To sustain life naturally

Green

To our surroundings do not be mean!
Do not litter, make it clean!
Plant trees make it green!

Earth is our shelter!
So, it is a must to make it better.
Its form and beauty must stay forever.
It is a God's creation always remember.

Blue

Bring back nature's hue,
Let her beauty replenishes anew,
This is for me and you.

Give water a chance,
To form waves, to dance,
Make it flow freely,
This for you and me.

Indigo

In your actions, be sincere, be true!
Nature relies on what you can do!
Nature really depends on you!

You need to start the chain of action,
Do this with determination,
Act now, do not hesitate,
Save nature, cooperate!

Violet

Do something to nature which you will not
regret!
Earth is suffering, please do not forget!
She needs you; she needs your help!

Please hear the Earth's cry,
Do not let her hopes die,
Do something for her protection,
For the entire wildlife and future generation.

THREE

To save the environment from its unwanted destruction, there are three questions that we need to focus on:

- *What to do?*
- *Who will act?*
- *When to begin?*

LOVE

L-isten to the needs of nature.
O-pen your heart, be the cure.
V-alley of care must be kept flowing.
E-arth will be saved, let love do the thing.

HOPE

H- umans can really do something.
O-ne at a time, start initiating.
P-ut a high hope on what we are doing.
E-very little thing will be saved if we start caring.

CARE

C-ome and let us prepare.
A-ll things must be planned with care.
R-ender enough time in thinking of solutions.
E-arth must be protected for the future
generation.

HELP

H-aving a heart for nature is a must.
E-nsure that care for animals will last.
L-end a hand for them to be safe.
P-rotect them, it is never too late.

TIME

T-ik-tok, time is running too fast!
I-nitiated moves, make them last!
M-ark your plan, put it into action!
E-nsure that everything will be for
wildlife protection!

LEAD

L-et your awareness initiates the motion.
E-nsure that love is the root of your actions.
A-lways remember that you need to take the stand.
D-efine the wildlife's future, lead the command.

POST

P-ublic must be well informed.
O-r else they will develop ignorance at all!
S-ocial media must be well used to make people aware.
T-echnology must be utilized to foster wildlife care.

FOUR

This chapter contains a poem of hope. The four-stanza poem about wildlife preservation received first place in the most creative category and most shared piece in the 2020 Earth Day from Home: Poetry Trends for ASEAN Wildlife.
The poem was heard nationwide over Radyo Balintataw and DZRH last June 2020

Call for Action

Oh! Earth, what a lovely place!
Its resources, we should not waste,
You and I must create protective chains,
To make its wildlife safe from emerging drastic
change.

Promote tree planting,
Stop animal poaching,
Coral reef destruction is not a good thing,
It is as bad as illegal mining.

Endangered plants and animals must be given
attention,
They should be loved by our generation,
We must plan and act for their full protection,
Let us make the future see the wildlife beyond
imagination.

ASEAN nations must work hand-in-hand,
Let initiative and cooperation lead the
command,
To make our world a better place,
For the entire wildlife and human race.

FIVE

For an artwork to be aesthetically pleasing, five basic elements of art need to be considered. Line, shape, color, texture, and space contribute to the way how the artwork communicates its message. These elements make a work of art interesting and worth appreciating.

"Rebirth"
by Rolaine San Juan

"Genesis 9:13"
by Rolaine San Juan

"City Lights in Land"
by Rolaine San Juan

"Unseen Truth"
by Rolaine San Juan

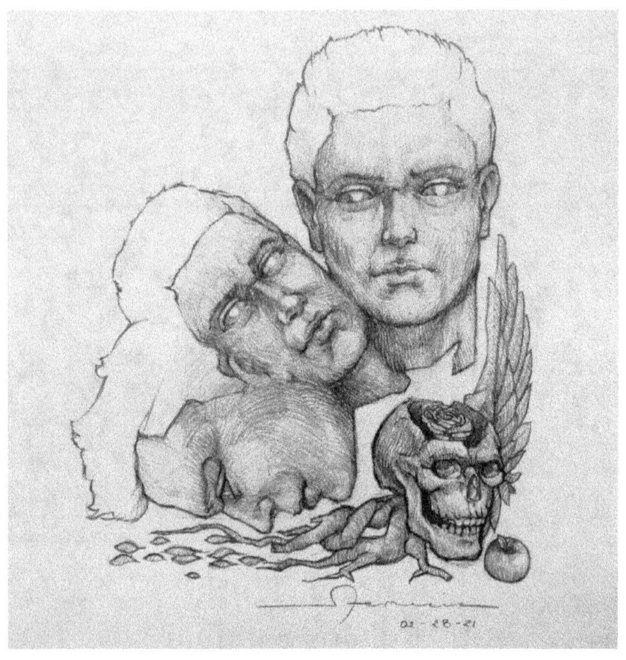

"Genetic Decoding"
by Nemesis Manahan

"Wise"
by Nemesis Manahan

"BiodiversiFree"
by Carlito Colinares

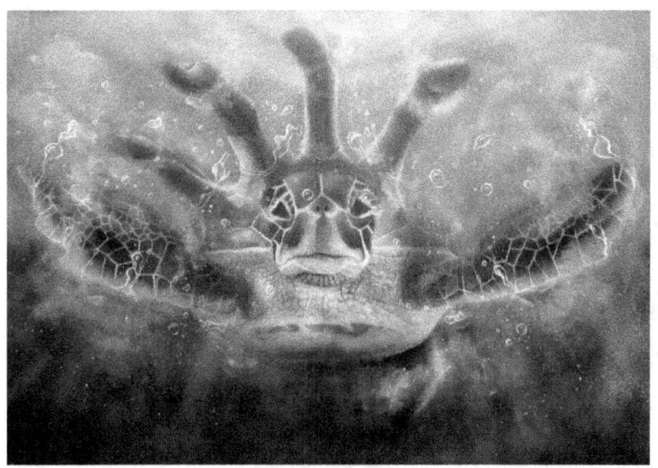

"Predator"
by Lyca Balume

"[PAG]dar[ASA] sa Bawat Pagpikit at Pagmulat ng Mata"
by Jonathan Tungol

SIX

The six letters of life will be revealed in this chapter. This is the site of one of the most important processes in nature that support the life of other living organisms – Photosynthesis.

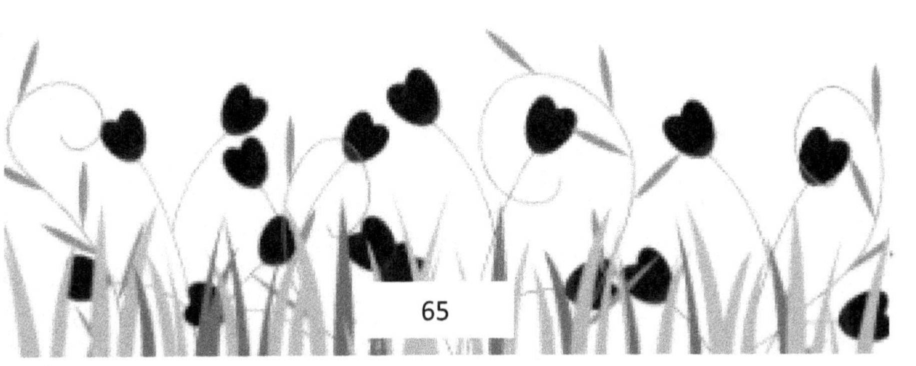

Life without Photosynthesis

Photosynthesis which occurs in the LEAVES is a natural chemical process wherein plants produce sugar (glucose) and oxygen (O_2) from carbon dioxide (CO_2) and water with the aid of light energy coming from the sun. Photosynthesis provides the necessary materials that living organisms need to survive. Oxygen as one of the products of the said process is very important for living organisms especially humans and animals to breathe.

Photosynthesis which is also referred to as the "food making process" produces foods necessary to living organisms. Foods serve as the living organisms' major source of energy which they use for their daily survival.

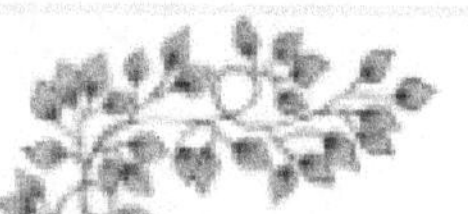

So how is life without photosynthesis? Think of this, a car without gasoline, a cellphone without a battery, and an ocean without water. Do you think the car, cellphone, and ocean would serve their purpose? If you say no, then you are right! Since photosynthesis is essential to life, without it, plants could not make food. Also, if there is no photosynthesis, plants would not be able to produce oxygen necessary for humans and animals to survive. With this, production of carbon dioxide will stop and in result will be the cause of plants' depletion. This can make extinction of other living organisms. If the scenario gets worst, the Earth which is known as the "The Planet of Life" would be lifeless and worthless.

As caretakers of the Earth and its systems, we the human beings must take initiative in protecting species that have vital roles in the process of photosynthesis. Greening activities like tree planting are very essential in promoting the essence of photosynthesis. 3R's must be promoted to reduce the number of factors that contribute to the decrease in number of plants.

The continuity of photosynthesis is in our hands! Thus, we must not stop thinking of ways on how photosynthesis will be in its continuous motion in supporting life. We can do something in taking out photosynthesis from being at risk!

SEVEN

The very reason why we need to take care of the environment is because God created it for us. Loving nature already means that we respect and love God. If we want God to be happy, let us do our part in taking good care of His masterpiece. Through this, the future generation can see how great God in creating the Earth, its resources, and its wonderful creatures.

Now, let us recall how God created everything 7 days through reading Genesis 1.

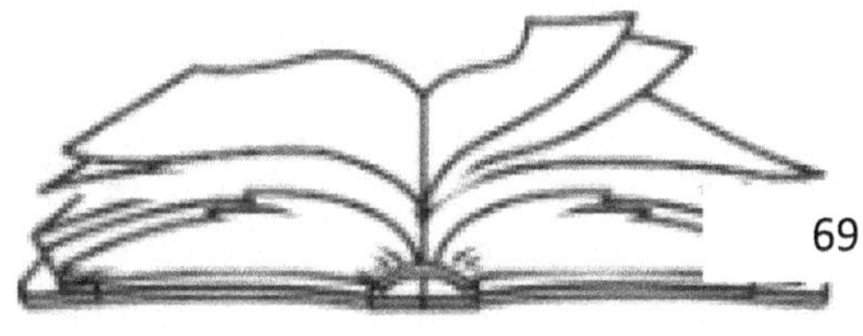

Genesis 1
King James Version

1 In the beginning God created the heaven and the earth.

² And the earth was without form, and void; and darkness was upon the face of the deep. And the Spirit of God moved upon the face of the waters.

³ And God said, Let there be light: and there was light.

⁴ And God saw the light, that it was good: and God divided the light from the darkness.

⁵ And God called the light Day, and the darkness he called Night. And the evening and the morning were the first day.

⁶ And God said, let there be a firmament in the midst of the waters, and let it divide the waters from the waters.

⁷ And God made the firmament, and divided the waters which were under the firmament from the waters which were above the firmament: and it was so.

⁸ And God called the firmament Heaven. And the evening and the morning were the second day.

⁹ And God said, Let the waters under the heaven be gathered unto one place, and let the dry land appear: and it was so.

¹⁰ And God called the dry land Earth; and the gathering of the waters called the Seas: and God saw that it was good.

¹¹ And God said, Let the earth bring forth grass, the herb yielding seed, and the fruit tree yielding fruit after his kind, whose seed is, upon the earth: and it was so.

¹² And the earth brought forth grass, and herb yielding seed after his kind, and the tree

yielding fruit, whose seed was, after his kind: and God saw that it was good.

13 And the evening and the morning were the third day.

14 And God said, let there be lights in the firmament of the heaven to divide the day from the night; and let them be for signs, and for seasons, and for days, and years:

15 And let them be for lights in the firmament of the heaven to give light upon the earth: and it was so.

16 And God made two great lights; the greater light to rule the day, and the lesser light to rule the night: he made the stars also.

17 And God set them in the firmament of the heaven to give light upon the earth,

18 And to rule over the day and over the night, and to divide the light from the darkness: and God saw that it was good.

19 And the evening and the morning were the fourth day.

20 And God said, Let the waters bring forth abundantly the moving creature that hath life, and fowl that may fly above the earth in the open firmament of heaven.

21 And God created great whales, and every living creature that moveth, which the waters brought forth abundantly, after their kind, and every winged fowl after his kind: and God saw that it was good.

22 And God blessed them, saying, be fruitful, and multiply, and fill the waters in the seas, and let fowl multiply in the earth.

23 And the evening and the morning were the fifth day.

24 And God said, Let the earth bring forth the living creature after his kind, cattle, and creeping thing, and beast of the earth after his kind: and it was so.

25 And God made the beast of the earth after his kind, and cattle after their kind, and everything that creepeth upon the earth after his kind: and God saw that it was good.

26 And God said, let us make man in our image, after our likeness: and let them have dominion over the fish of the sea, and over the fowl of the air, and over the cattle, and over all the earth, and over every creeping thing that creepeth upon the earth.

27 So God created man in his own image, in the image of God created he him; male and female created he them.

28 And God blessed them, and God said unto them, be fruitful, and multiply, and replenish the earth, and subdue it: and have dominion over the fish of the sea, and over the fowl of the air, and over every living thing that moveth upon the earth.

²⁹ And God said, Behold, I have given you every herb bearing seed, which is upon the face of all the earth, and every tree, in the which is the fruit of a tree yielding seed; to you it shall be for meat.

³⁰ And to every beast of the earth, and to every fowl of the air, and to everything that creepeth upon the earth, wherein there is life, I have given every green herb for meat: and it was so.

³¹ And God saw everything that he had made, and behold, it was very good. And the evening and the morning were the sixth day.

EIGHT

This chapter consists of eight more verses about nature. Read each. These verses may help you realize that God created everything in nature so; we must protect, conserve, and save all His creations.

Revelation 4:11

"Worthy are You, our Lord and our God, to receive glory and honor and power; for You created all things, and because of Your will they existed, and were created."

Genesis 2:4-9

This is the account of the heavens and the earth when they were created, in the day that the Lord God made earth and heaven. Now no shrub of the field was yet in the earth, and no plant of the field had yet sprouted, for the Lord God had not sent rain upon the earth, and there was no man to cultivate the ground. But a mist used to rise from the earth and water the whole surface of the ground.

Psalm 104:14-16

He causes the grass to grow for the
cattle,
And vegetation for the labor of man,
So that he may bring forth food from the
earth,
And wine which makes man's heart
glad,
So that he may make his face glisten
with oil,
And food which sustains man's heart.
The trees of the Lord drink their fill,
The cedars of Lebanon which He
planted.

Leviticus 26:4

Then I will give you rain in due season, and the land shall yield her increase, and the trees of the field shall yield their fruit.

Jeremiah 27:5

"I have made the earth, the men and the beasts which are on the face of the earth by My great power and by My outstretched arm, and I will give it to the one who is pleasing in My sight.

Isaiah 45:12

"It is I who made the earth and created man upon it.
I stretched out the heavens with My hands. And I ordained all their host.

Job 12:7-10

"But now ask the beasts and let them teach you.
And the birds of the heavens and let them tell you.
"Or speak to the earth, and let it teach you.
And let the fish of the sea declare to you.
"Who among all these does not know.
That the hand of the Lord has done this, read more.
In whose hand is the life of every living thing,
And the breath of all mankind?

Acts 14:15

"Men, why are you doing these things? We are also men of the same nature as you and preach the gospel to you that you should turn from these vain things to a living God, who made the heaven and the earth and the sea and all that is in them.

Reader's Reflection

About The Author

Dr. Jan Michael C. Sotto is currently holding a Public Secondary School Head Teacher III position in Lolomboy National High School. He is also working as a Part-Time Professor in Jesus Is Lord Colleges Foundation Inc. and Mt. Carmel Colle in Bocaue, Bulacan, teaching education and Science-related subjects. He earned his degree in Master of Arts in Science Education in PHINMA-Araullo University, Cabanatuan City, Nueva Ecija in April 2018, several years after he completed the Academic Requirements in Master of Secondary Education Major in Chemistry at Bulacan State University, Malolos City, Bulacan. With a dream of serving the academe and the community efficiently, he is currently taking a

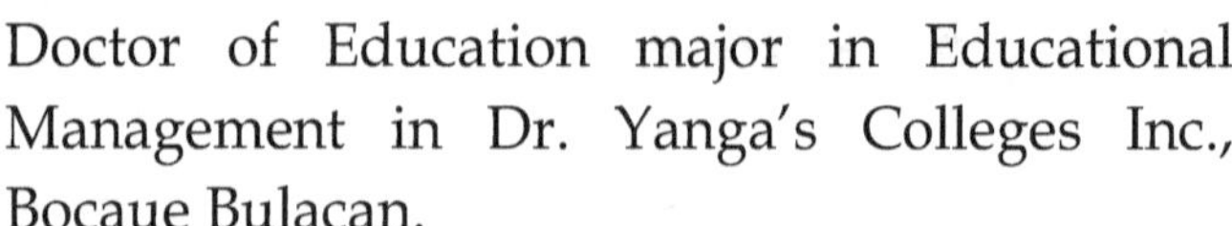

Doctor of Education major in Educational Management in Dr. Yanga's Colleges Inc., Bocaue Bulacan.

Sir JM, as he is fondly called, received several awards in the field of Education. He was awarded as the Most Outstanding Teacher in the Municipality of Bocaue in October 2016 during World Teachers' Day celebration. In the same year, he received Gawad Galing Bocaue – Outstanding Educator Award during the Rizal Day celebration. He was awarded as one of the Most Outstanding Teachers in the Philippines by Instabright Publication on January 11, 2020, at the Tagaytay Convention Center. At the school level, he received certificates of recognition for four consecutive years for having an IPCRF rating under the outstanding category. Recently, he became one of the recipients of the Gawad Ybarra Awards for Educators by Theophany University and Asia Global Heroes Award by Asian+Council of Leaders, Administrators, Deans, and Educators In Business (ACLADEB).

Sir JM is leaving significant marks in the field of social and community development. At present, he manages two non-government groups, the Project Go 100 and BEAGIVER-

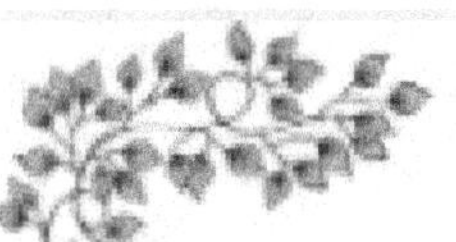

Bulacan. Both groups are active in doing community projects.

In the field of teaching, he was able to make a name in the field of research and innovation. In the 2018 Division Science and Technology Fair, he bagged 2nd place in Science Strategic Intervention Materials Making. This is his fourth recognition after he placed 3rd in the 2013 EDDIS level On-the-Spot Improvisation, 9th in the 2013 level On-the-Spot Improvisation, and 5th in 2011 Division Science Strategic Intervention Materials Making. In research, he represented Region III in the 2011 National Science Quest – Investigatory Project Making – Teacher Category after he won 1st Runner-up in the Regional Level and Champion in the Division Level.

In the field of literary arts, JM became a contributor in the Municipality of Bocaue's Publication "Bocaue Ngayon", Lolomboy National High School's Official Newspaper "Ang Pagoda" and Storybook Org Philippines' Open Learning Resource Website. Last 2020, he participated in different online poem writing contests, and with his creativity and imagination, he was able to win First Place in the 2020 Earth Day from Home: Poetry Trends for ASEAN Wildlife, an international poem

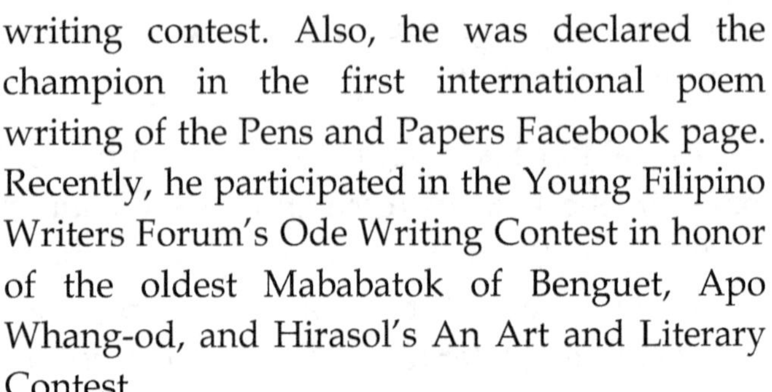

writing contest. Also, he was declared the champion in the first international poem writing of the Pens and Papers Facebook page. Recently, he participated in the Young Filipino Writers Forum's Ode Writing Contest in honor of the oldest Mababatok of Benguet, Apo Whang-od, and Hirasol's An Art and Literary Contest.

References

Eight Bible Verses

https://bible.knowing-jesus.com/topics/Nature?fbclid=IwAR0aWny-cC5EoxZTvsYAvGth6nO6Z9_616E_7XTsVMno CHPpVmpHVQ-lyw

Five Elements of Art

https://www.widewalls.ch/magazine/five-elements-of-art

Genesis 1

https://www.biblegateway.com/passage/?search=Genesis%201&version=KJV